To Carnival!

A Celebration in Saint Lucia

WRITTEN BY Baptiste Paul

ILLUSTRATED BY Jana Glatt

Barefoot Books

"Manjé! Eat, Melba!" calls Manman Lucy. "Tomorrow's a big day!"

The grown-ups make plans for morning. Carnival!
Melba tries to listen, but her mind wanders...

Soca music thumps and steel pan clanks.
People dance in feathery costumes. Judges crown winners.
Melba breathes in smells — fried bakes and chicken smothered in
green seasoning. Mmmmm...

"Melba? Did you hear?"
Manman Lucy's voice draws
Melba back to the porch. Melba nods.
"Hurry to bed or you won't
wake up in time."

"Bonswè!" Melba slides under the net, but her eyes won't close! Her excitement churns like the sea until the moon is high in the sky.

When Melba wakes, sunshine spills through the window.
The house is quiet.
Too quiet.

"Where is everybody?"

"In town," yawns cousin Zarah, feeding the baby. "Tonton said anyone who wanted a ride had to leave by seven o'clock."

A lump as hard as a sea grape forms in Melba's throat. "But Tonton chose *my* idea for their band's costume! I need to see if they win!"

"Relax," Zarah says. "He left bus money."

One excited girl heads out the door, with two E.C. dollars in hand.

"To carnival!"

Along the road, everything reminds Melba of Carnival. The sound of steel pan music returns. **tink-a-tink-tink! tink-a-tink-tink!**

Melba stops. It isn't a dream … it's Misyé Francois!

"Bonjou! Come hear my song.
It's about a mannikou who wakes
in the day and sleeps at night," he says.
Melba chuckles. Mannikou are nocturnal!
"I have to catch a bus to Carnival."

Misyé Francois bursts into song, rubber-tipped hammers in hand. He clunks on the steel pan. **tink-a-tink-tink!** Melba's feet can't resist. Look! A mannikou pokes out his head!

Everyone is jamming
when Melba hears the growl
of a bus. V-V-VROOM!
"Too late, it's gone!" she cries.
"Relax," says Misyé Francois.
"Let's walk to the next bus stop."

One excited girl,

a steel pan drummer

and a mannikou

hurry down the mountain.

"To Carnival!"

Before the bus stop, Melba spots two green jacquot and a rainbow in the canopy.

"Help!" cries a voice. "My kite is stuck," says her friend Kenwin. "Can you help?"

"Let the jacquot untangle it," Melba jokes. "I've got to catch a bus to Carnival."

"I'll let you fly my kite."

Melba's face lights up. Fly a kite! "All right!"

Melba frees the kite. On the climb down, a whirring noise catches her ears. "The bus! Oh no, not again."

Taillights zoom out of sight. "*Relax*," says Kenwin. "Miss Drina has a truck."

One excited girl,

a steel pan drummer,

one mannikou,

two jacquot

and a boy with a kite

hurry down the mountain.

"To Carnival!"

Melba passes guava, papaya and golden apple trees. Finally, she spots large, long leaves. Banana trees! She sees Miss Drina, the banana farmer, placing bunches into boxes.

"Bonjou! We missed the bus to Carnival," Melba explains. "Will you drive us?"

"Sorry," Miss Drina says. "Truck's broken."

"Oh no, this can't be!" cries Melba.

"Relax," says Miss Drina. "If you help me fill these boxes, you can have a banana while we walk together."

Melba lifts a box. Something moves. She peers through the holes and sees blue, black and yellow — just like the flag!

"That's Maria the zanndoli," says Miss Drina. "We rescued her. Once she's healthy, we'll bring her home." Miss Drina points through a clearing and Melba realizes they're close to the town!

One excited girl,

a steel pan drummer,

a mannikou,

two jacquot,

a boy with a kite,

a banana farmer,

four boxes of bananas

and a zanndoli

hurry down the mountain.

"To Carnival!"

When they reach the town square, Melba spots the end
of the parade. "No! That's the last band. It's over!"
   Everyone stops. Shoulders slump.
One excited girl becomes one
disappointed girl.

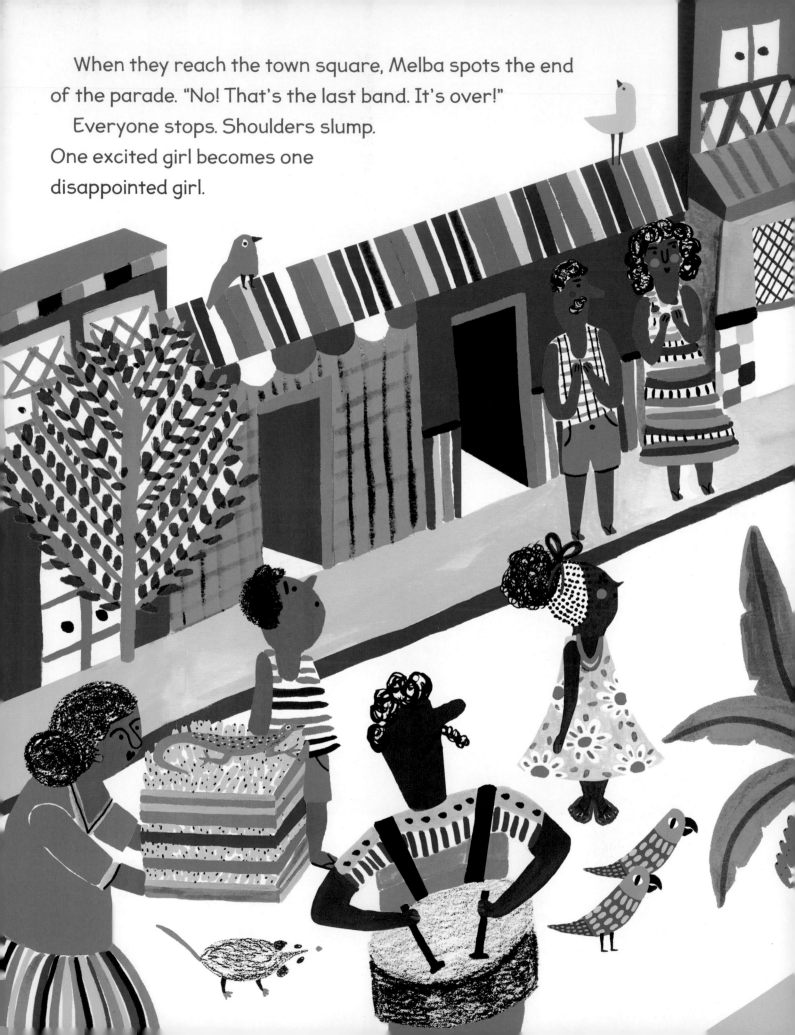

"Re-e-e-lax," sings Misyé Francois.
Melba turns to see the lively trail of
friends following her. "You know... maybe
we didn't miss out after all!"

Her band waves, "*We* are a parade!"
The crowds cheer.

As one excited girl,

a steel pan drummer,

a mannikou,

two jacquot,

a boy with a kite,

a banana farmer,

four boxes
of bananas

and a zanndoli

march their wacky band down Main Street.

Melba spots Tonton's band in the square.
The costumes look great!
  Tonton shakes his head. "We didn't win.
You must be disappointed."
  Melba laughs. "Re-e-e-lax!

   . . . There's always next year."

creole Pronunciation and Glossary

bakes (BAYKS): fried, round bread

bonjou (boh-JOO): hello

bonswè (boh-SWAY): good night

E.C. (EE-SEE): Eastern Caribbean dollars (the local money)

jacquot (ZHA-ko): a green parrot that is the national bird of Saint Lucia

manjé (mah-ZHAY): eat!

Manman (mah-mah): Mother

mannikou (MAN-uh-coo): opossum

Misyé (meh-SEWR): Mister

soca (SOH-kah): fast, upbeat music that is a mix of reggae and calypso

Tonton (toh-toh): Uncle

zanndoli (ZAN-doh-lee): a whiptail lizard that is blue, black, yellow and white like the Saint Lucian flag

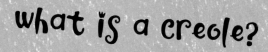

what is a creole?

A creole is a combination of different languages. People who speak different languages begin to communicate with one another using words from more than one language, which creates a whole new language. Saint Lucian Creole (also called Kwéyòl) is a mix of French with various West African languages, English and Carib.

Did you know...

Every year on Easter Monday, a **kite-flying festival** is held in Saint Lucia. Traditional handmade kites are made of paper and bamboo sticks.

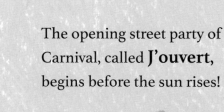

The opening street party of Carnival, called **J'ouvert**, begins before the sun rises!

Steel pan drums were first developed in the 1930s in Trinidad, but the cultural practice of drumming was brought to the islands by enslaved Africans in the 1700s.

where in the world is Saint Lucia?

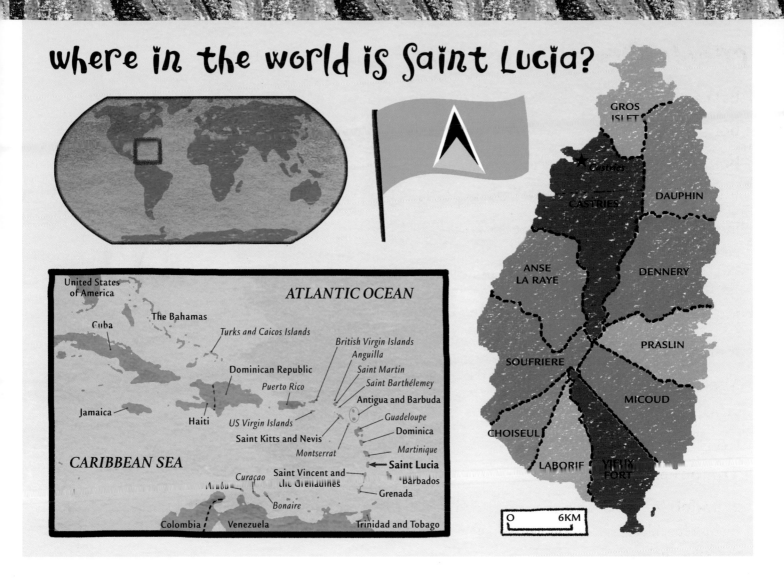

what is carnival?

Why do people celebrate Carnival?

Carnival began as a time to feast and celebrate before Lent. The Catholic season of Lent is a time of sacrifice, or giving up things you normally enjoy, like some foods. Today, people of all faiths enjoy Carnival as a celebration of community and traditional cultures.

What do people do at Carnival in Saint Lucia?

The days of Carnival are filled with parties, parades, competitions for music and dancing, jump-ups (street parties) and fish fries. Joining the parade is called "playing mas." Groups of people called "mas bands" dress in elaborate outfits decked in feathers, jewels and beads and compete for prizes for the best costumes.

Where else in the world do people celebrate Carnival?

Carnival is celebrated in over fifty countries around the world! Some of the biggest, most famous carnivals happen in Rio de Janeiro (Brazil), New Orleans (USA) and Venice (Italy). Other countries in Central and South America, the Caribbean Islands, parts of Africa and Europe as well as the southern United States celebrate Carnival too. There are always parades, music and street foods, but each has their own local traditions.

Author's note

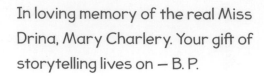

As a child, I loved it when the Carnival season got underway. The smell of grilled chicken marinated in green seasoning got my taste buds excited. I enjoyed watching the creative costumes on display, but the best part was the calypso and soca music. How I dreamed of playing mas in the Carnival parade! My family couldn't afford the costumes, so I watched from the sidelines. But the sense of unity and community while celebrating our culture is the true spirit of Carnival.

To the children of Saint Lucia and surrounding islands: dream big!

— **Baptiste Paul**

In loving memory of the real Miss Drina, Mary Charley. Your gift of storytelling lives on — B. P.

To my daughter Malú, who was in my belly while I was making this book. In the future I will be able to show her this book made with love — J. G.

Illustrator's note

Carnival here in Brazil is very similar to Carnival in Saint Lucia, with bright, feathered costumes and parades. The biggest difference is the music: in Brazil, we play samba. Creating the costumes for Carnival is always exciting and illustrating costumes for this book was exciting too! I like to make art that is bright and textured, using the diversity of the world as the biggest inspiration for my art. I hope this book conveys the beauty and magic of Carnival!

— **Jana Glatt**

Barefoot Books
Bradford Mill, 23 Bradford Street
West Concord, MA 01742

Barefoot Books
29/30 Fitzroy Square
London, W1T 6LQ

Text copyright © 2021 by Baptiste Paul
Illustrations copyright © 2021 by Jana Glatt
The moral rights of Baptiste Paul and Jana Glatt have been asserted

First published in United States of America by Barefoot Books, Inc
and in Great Britain by Barefoot Books, Ltd in 2021

Graphic design by Sarah Soldano, Barefoot Books
Edited and art directed by Kate DePalma, Barefoot Books
Reproduction by Bright Arts, Hong Kong. Printed in China on 100% acid-free paper
This book was typeset in Athelas, Chelsea Market Pro, JollyGood Proper, Kingdom and Minya Nouvelle
The illustrations were prepared in liquid water-based paint, pencils and crayon

Hardback ISBN 978-1-64686-161-3 | Paperback ISBN 978-1-64686-162-0
E-book ISBN 978-1-64686-251-1
Spanish paperback ISBN 978-1-64686-215-3
French paperback ISBN 978-1-64686-216-0

British Cataloguing-in-Publication Data: a catalogue record
for this book is available from the British Library

Library of Congress Cataloging-in-Publication Data
is available under LCCN 2020949756

135798642